DARK HUNTER

THE HOUSE OF MEMORIES

Cover design: Dan Bramall. Cover photo: Shutterstock.

Main body text set in Times LT Std. 14/22
Typeface provided by Adobe Systems.

Darby Creek
A division of Lerner Publishing Group, Inc.
241 First Avenue North
Minneapolis, MN 55401 USA

For reading levels and more information, look up this title at
www.lernerbooks.com.

Library of Congress Cataloging-in-Publication Data

Hulme-Cross, Benjamin.
    The house of memories / by Benjamin Hulme-Cross. — American edition.
       pages cm. — (Dark Hunter)
    Summary: Dark Hunter Mr. Blood leaves Edgar and Mary at an empty house
  where they encounter an evil spider woman who may be tied to their past.
    ISBN 978-1-4677-5722-5 (lb : alk. paper) — ISBN 978-1-4677-8085-8 (pb : alk.
  paper) — ISBN 978-1-4677-8657-7 (eb pdf : alk. paper)
    [1. Spiders—Fiction. 2. Demonology—Fiction. 3. Supernatural—Fiction.
  4. Horror stories.] I. Title.
  PZ7.1.H86Hou 2015
  [Fic]—dc23   2015002263

Manufactured in the United States of America
3 – DOC – 12/1/15

DARK HUNTER

THE HOUSE OF MEMORIES

BENJAMIN HULME-CROSS

ILLUSTRATED BY NELSON EVERGREEN

darbycreek

MINNEAPOLIS

The Dark Hunter

Mr. Daniel Blood is the Dark Hunter.
People call him to fight evil demons,
vampires, and ghosts.

Edgar and Mary help Mr. Blood
with his work.

The three hunters need to be strong and
clever to survive . . .

Contents

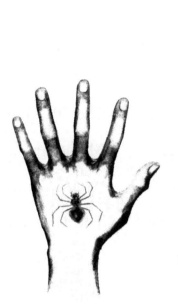

Chapter 1

The Old House

The old house in the woods was falling apart. Twisted trees grew all around it. The roof was almost hidden by brown moss. The door hung off the doorframe. It had cobwebs all over it.

The house was rotting away.

Edgar, Mary, and Mr. Blood stood in front of the house. Edgar wasn't happy.

"Mr. Blood, why are you leaving us on our own again?" Edgar said. "How long are you going to be away this time?"

"I'll be back in the morning," Mr. Blood said. "I need to go alone."

"But why can't we come with you?" asked Mary. "Are you trying to keep us safe from something?"

"Yes, that's it," said Mr. Blood. "I don't want to drag you into danger."

"But you've often put us in danger before!" said Edgar.

"You will have lots to think about while you wait for me," said Mr. Blood. "I know that you don't remember anything from when you were little children. Why don't you try to remember where you got those tattoos?"

Mary looked at the small spider tattoo on the back of her left hand. It was itchy. She scratched it.

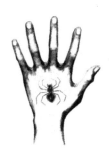

Edgar stared at his spider tattoo, and a chill ran down his spine.

"Have we been to this house before?" he asked.

"Of course not!" said Mr. Blood. But Edgar didn't believe him.

"I'll go now," Mr. Blood said. "There's food in the bag. When it gets dark, stay inside. And whatever you do . . ."

Mary knew what he was going to say. "Don't let anyone in!"

"Good," said Mr. Blood. "I'll be back by dawn."

Mr. Blood waved good-bye, turned, and walked into the woods.

Edgar and Mary stood in front of
the house. This time, it was Mary who
shivered. She was scared too.

"I think we *have* been here before," she
said. She reached out to touch the door.
It creaked open.

Chapter 2

Memories

It was dark inside the house.

Edgar lit his torch. There was just one big room, with a roof on top. Its floor was bare earth. There were thick cobwebs on the walls.

"It's lucky we don't mind spiders!" said Edgar.

"I'm not scared of spiders. But this is awful. Let's clean up a bit," Mary said.

She grabbed a broom that was lying on the ground. They both swept away the cobwebs.

"That's odd," Mary said. "There are lots of cobwebs, but I can't see any spiders. I wonder where they are."

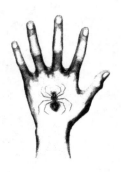

Edgar said, "I'm glad they aren't in here. Don't go looking for them."

Mary scratched her hand again.

"And stop doing that," Edgar said. "You're making my tattoo itch too." He rubbed the tattoo on his hand.

"Come on, let's sit down and have some of our food," he said.

There was a small table and two chairs next to the single tiny window. Mary and Edgar sat down and looked at each other.

"I feel very odd," Edgar said.

"So do I," said Mary. "I feel like I can almost remember something. From when we were little. A bad thing."

"Me too," Edgar said.

"We have been in this house before. I'm sure of it," said Mary.

"So am I," Edgar said. "But I don't know when."

The two of them sat, both thinking hard. Outside, it was very dark.

On the roof of the house, something as black as the night began to crawl down the chimney.

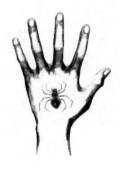

Chapter 3

Arak

Mary looked up. She saw a very old woman standing in the middle of the room.

Mary screamed.

Edgar turned to look. He felt the hairs on his neck stand on end.

The old woman didn't say anything.

Then Edgar and Mary both spoke at the same time.

"Who are you?" said Edgar.

"What do you want?" said Mary.

The woman stepped forward. She had long white hairs hanging over her face. *Just like cobwebs*, thought Edgar.

The old woman smiled. She had cracked lips and broken, rotting teeth.

"My name is Arak," the old woman said. "It's nice to see you, my dears. I don't get many visitors. I live here."

Mary said, "You weren't here when we came in. Where were you?"

"Outside," said Arak. "You didn't hear me come in. I don't make much noise. It's easier to live in the forest if you keep quiet."

"It's easier to creep up on people too!" said Mary.

"And what about you?" asked the old woman. "Why are you two lovely children alone in the forest?"

"Oh, we're not alone . . ." began Edgar. Mary stamped on his foot to make him stop talking. "Ow!" he said.

"We just like to explore," said Mary. "We should go now."

The old woman's eyes went narrow.

"Oh, my dears, you must not go into the forest at night," she said. "That's not a good idea. You must stay here with me. We have so much to talk about."

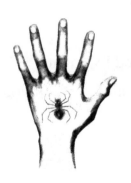

Chapter 4

The Truth

Mary felt scared. "We have to go," she said. "We don't know you."

"Don't you?" said Arak. "I think you do."

She turned to Edgar. "Edgar, you said there was someone with you. Who is he?"

Mary stared at her. "Edgar didn't say
it was a man. And how do you know
Edgar's name?"

Arak didn't answer that. She said,
"Do you remember this house, my dears?"

"We think we have been here before.
But we don't know when," Edgar said.

"I'm glad you remember," said Arak.
"Now, tell me about the man who left you
here."

"He didn't leave us!" Mary shouted.

"Yes, he did. We're here, and he's not,"
Edgar said.

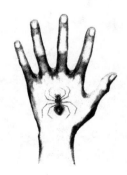

Arak said, "Is this man Mr. Blood, the Dark Hunter?"

Edgar nodded.

"I thought so," said Arak. "Listen, my dears. Mr. Blood is not what you think. He says he is a good man. But as long as you are with him, you are in danger."

Edgar thought about all the evil beasts and monsters that Mr. Blood had fought. It was true. He and Mary were always in danger.

"You still haven't told us how you know about us," said Mary.

The old woman gave her a kind look. "Sit down, my dear. I will tell you the truth about you and Mr. Blood now. But it will be hard for you to hear it."

Mary did not sit. "I don't want to listen to you," she said. "Mr. Blood is like our father."

Edgar said, "Let's hear what she has to say. What harm can it do?"

"Edgar, this doesn't feel right," Mary said. "Something bad is going on. We should leave."

Edgar was angry. "I want to know what Arak has to say! I'm staying."

"If Mary wants to leave, we must let her," said Arak. "I don't want to keep her here against her will."

Then Arak gave a shrill laugh. "Not that I could do that, of course. I'm only a poor old woman."

Mary ran to the door and pulled it open.

Then she screamed.

Chapter 5

Trapped

Mr. Blood stood a few steps away from the house.

He was still as a stone. It was as if he had frozen as he ran toward the house. Mary knew he was under a spell.

"What have you done to him?" Mary turned to Arak. "It was you, wasn't it? You put a spell on him. Who are you? What do you want from us?"

Arak said nothing. She began to walk in slow circles around Edgar's chair.

40

Edgar tried to get up. But his legs and arms would not move. He could only sit still and stare at her.

It must be a spell! He felt like a fly in a spider's web.

As she walked, Arak began to talk.

"Years ago, I took care of two small children. You two children. I fed you and I loved you and I taught you. I taught you to be strong. You were very strong," she said, looking at Mary.

"And I taught you to listen to your feelings. That was your gift, my dear." She touched Edgar's cheek.

"I don't know what you mean," Mary said.

"Look at my hand," said Arak.

On the back of Arak's left hand was a small tattoo of a spider. It was just the same as the tattoos on Edgar and Mary's hands.

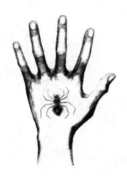

The old woman kept talking. "One day a wicked man called Mr. Blood stole my two dear children from me. At last I have got you back."

"No!" Mary shouted. She ran out of the door, toward Mr. Blood.

"He can't help you, my dear. I've made sure of that!" Arak smiled at Edgar. She looked very evil. "Did you know, some spiders eat their own children?"

Outside the house, Mary shook
Mr. Blood. He didn't move. She didn't
know how to break the spell.

Mr. Blood was holding a sack in his
hand. Mary took a closer look at it.
Something in the sack moved.

She pulled Mr. Blood's fingers open
and took the sack.

"He can't help you. Edgar can't help you either," Arak called to Mary. "Don't you think it's time you came back inside?"

Mary walked back into the house. Edgar sat frozen in his chair.

It looked as if Arak had gone. Mary looked around. She could not see her anywhere.

But she saw something else.

Mary's blood ran cold, and she dropped the sack onto Edgar's lap.

Something huge was coming out of a dark corner.

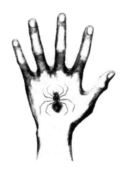

Chapter 6

Spider

The thing was very big. It had long, thin legs like broomsticks. Its body looked like a mass of black bristles. It had small red eyes and two long, curved, black fangs.

It was a giant spider.

The spider came toward Mary.
Its hairy legs scraped on the floor as it
moved.

"I'm glad you came back, my dear!"
The monster spoke with Arak's voice.
Arak was not a person—she was a spider
demon!

Mary couldn't speak. Just like Edgar
and Mr. Blood, she was under Arak's
spell. They were all trapped like flies in
the spider's web.

Arak the spider came to the table. Edgar's eyes were wide with fear.

The spider laughed. "Who shall I eat first?" she asked. Neither of the children could speak. "I think I will begin with Edgar."

Mary began to cry.

Arak's two front legs reached out until they scraped against the table. Her sharp fangs were very close to Edgar's face.

"You two are mine!" Arak hissed.

Something hissed back at her.

Mr. Blood's sack was still on Edgar's lap. Something shot out of it, like an arrow. It was a snake.

Arak had no time to move away. The snake hit her in the head. It sunk its fangs between her eyes.

She screamed. Her legs thrashed around, knocking Edgar over.

The snake kept biting. Arak began to slow down. The snake's bite was killing her.

Arak's spell broke as she died. Edgar and Mary could move again.

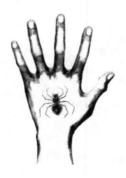

The door opened. Mr. Blood was outside. The spell on him was broken too.

Edgar and Mary ran past him, out of the door and out into the night.

Chapter 7

Later

Mary and Edgar waited in the woods for Mr. Blood.

Some time later, Mr. Blood came out of the house. He went up to the children. For a long while they stood still without saying anything.

Mr. Blood spoke first. "Arak lied to you. She wasn't like a mother to you. She had a spell on you both. She wanted to make you her slaves. I broke the spell and took you away. She hated me for that."

"Why did you bring us back here?" Edgar asked.

"She still had power over you both," said Mr. Blood. "Now you are free."

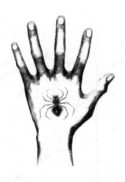

"I know this was hard for you," Mr. Blood told them. "But we all have to face our own demons one day. I thought you were ready to face Arak."

Edgar and Mary looked up at the Dark Hunter. He smiled at them.

"And I was right," he said.